melville house classics

THE DEVIL

THE DEVIL

LEO TOLSTOY

TRANSLATED BY LOUISE AND AYLMER MAUDE

MELVILLEHOUSE
BROOKLYN, NEW YORK

MELVILLE HOUSE PUBLISHING
145 PLYMOUTH STREET
BROOKLYN, NEW YORK 11201
MHPBOOKS.COM

FIRST MELVILLE HOUSE PRINTING: 2004

ISBN: 978-0-9746078-3-2

PRINTED IN THE UNITED STATES OF AMERICA

 2 3 4 5 6 7 8 9 10

LIBRARY OF CONGRESS CATALOGING-IN-PUBLICATION DATA

TOLSTOY, LEO, GRAF, 1828–1910
   [DYAVOL. ENGLISH]
   THE DEVIL / BY LEO TOLSTOY ; TRANSLATED BY LOUISE AND
AYLMER MAUDE
     P. CM.
   ISBN 978-0-9746078-3-2
   I. MAUDE, LOUISE SHANKS, 1855–1939. II. MAUDE, AYLMER,
1858–1938. III. TITLE.
   PG3366.D6 2004
   891.73'3--DC22
                          2004008000

THE DEVIL

But I say unto you, that every one that looketh on a woman to lust after her hath committed adultery with her already in his heart.

And if thy right eye causeth thee to stumble, pluck it out, and cast it from thee: for it is profitable for thee that one of thy members should perish, and not thy whole body be cast into hell.

And if thy right hand causeth thee to stumble, cut it off, and cast it from thee: for it is profitable for thee that one of thy members should perish, and not thy whole body go into hell.

—MATTHEW V. 28–30

I A brilliant career lay before Yevgeny Irtenev. He had everything necessary to attain it: an admirable education at home, high honours when he graduated in law at Petersburg University, and connexions in the highest society through his recently deceased father; he had also already begun service in one of the Ministries under the protection of the minister. Moreover he had a fortune; even a large one, though insecure. His father had lived abroad and in Petersburg, allowing his sons, Yevgeny and Andrey (who was older than Yevgeny and in the Horse Guards), six thousand rubles a year each, while he himself and his wife spent a great deal. He only used to visit his estate for a couple of months in summer and did not concern himself with its direction, entrusting it all to an unscrupulous manager who also failed to attend to it, but in whom he had complete confidence.

After the father's death, when the brothers began to divide the property, so many debts were discovered that their lawyer even advised them to refuse the inheritance and retain only an estate left them by their grandmother, which was valued at a hundred thousand rubles. But a neighbouring landed-proprietor who had done business with old Irtenev, that is to say, who had promissory notes from him and had come to Petersburg on that account, said that in spite of the debts they could straighten out affairs so as to retain a large fortune (it would only be necessary to sell the forest and some outlying land, retaining the rich Semyonov estate with four thousand *desyatins* of black earth, the sugar factory, and two hundred *desyatins* of water-meadows) if one devoted oneself to the management of the estate, settled there, and farmed it wisely and economically.

And so, having visited the estate in spring (his father had died in Lent), Yevgeny looked into everything, resolved to retire from the Civil Service, settle in the country with his mother, and undertake the management with the object of preserving the main estate. He arranged with his brother, with whom he was very friendly, that he would pay him either four thousand rubles a year, or a lump sum of eighty thousand, for which Andrey would hand over to him his share of his inheritance. So he arranged matters and, having settled down with his mother in the big house, began managing the estate eagerly, yet cautiously.

It is generally supposed the Conservatives are usually old people, and that those in favour of change are the young. That is not quite correct. Usually Conservatives are young people: those who want to live but who do not think about how to live, and have not time to think, and therefore take as a model for themselves a way of life that they have seen. Thus it was with Yevgeny. Having settled in the village, his aim and ideal was to restore the form of life that had existed, not in his father's time—his father had been a bad manager—but in his grandfather's. And now he tried to resurrect the general spirit of his grandfather's life—in the house, the garden, and in the estate management—of course with changes suited to the times—everything on a large scale—good order, method, and everybody satisfied. But to do this entailed much work. It was necessary to meet the demands of the creditors and the banks, and for that purpose to sell some land and arrange renewals of credit. It was also necessary to get money to carry on (partly by farming out land, and partly by hiring labour) the immense operations on the Semyonov estate, with its four hundred *desyatins* of ploughland and its sugar factory, and to deal with the garden so that it should not seem to be neglected or in decay.

There was much work to do, but Yevgeny had plenty of strength, physical and mental. He was twenty-six, of medium height, strongly built, with muscles developed by gymnastics. He was fullblooded and his whole neck was very red, his teeth and lips were bright, and his hair soft and curly though not thick. His only physical defect was short-sightedness, which he had himself developed by using spectacles, so that he could not now do without a pince-nez, which had already formed a line on the bridge of his nose.

Such was he physically. For his spiritual portrait it might be said that the better people knew him the better they liked him. His mother had always loved him more than anyone else, and now after her husband's death she concentrated on him not only her whole affection but her whole life. Nor was it only his mother who so loved him. All his comrades at the high school and the university not merely liked him very much, but respected him. He had this effect on all who met him. It was impossible not to believe what he said, impossible to suspect any deception or falseness in one who had such an open, honest face and in particular such eyes.

In general his personality helped him much in his affairs. A creditor who would have refused another trusted him. The clerk, the village Elder, or a peasant, who would have played a dirty trick and cheated someone else, forgot to deceive under the pleasant impression of intercourse with this kindly, agreeable, and above all candid man. It was the end of May. Yevgeny had somehow managed in town to get the vacant land freed from the mortgage, so as to sell it to a merchant, and had borrowed money from that same merchant to replenish his stock, that is to say, to procure horses, bulls, and carts, and in particular to begin to build a necessary farm-house. The matter had been arranged. The timber was being carted, the carpenters were already at work, and manure for the estate was being brought on eighty carts, but everything still hung by a thread.

II Amid these cares something came about which, though unimportant, tormented Yevgeny at the time. As a young man he had lived as all healthy young men live, that is, he had had relations with women of various kinds. He was not a libertine but neither, as he himself said, was he a monk. He only turned to this, however, in so far as was necessary for physical health and to have his mind free, as he used to say. This had begun when he was sixteen and had gone on satisfactorily—in the sense that he had never given himself up to debauchery, never once been infatuated, and had never contracted a disease. At first he had a seamstress in Petersburg, then she got spoilt and he made other arrangements, and that side of his affairs was so well secured that it did not trouble him. But now he was living in the country for the second month and did not at all know what he was to do. Compulsory self-restraint was beginning to have a bad effect on him.

Must he really go to town for that purpose? And where to? How? That was the only thing that disturbed him; but as he was convinced that the thing was necessary and that he needed it, it really became a necessity, and he felt that he was not free and that his eyes involuntarily followed every young woman.

He did not approve of having relations with a married woman or a maid in his own village. He knew by report that both his father and grandfather had been quite different in this matter from other landowners of

that time. At home they had never had any entangle-
ments with peasant-women, and he had decided that he
would not do so either; but afterwards, feeling himself
ever more and more under compulsion and imagining
with horror what might happen to him in the neighbouring country town, and reflecting on the fact that
the days of serfdom were now over, he decided that it
might be done on the spot. Only it must be done so
that no one should know of it, and not for the sake of
debauchery but merely for health's sake—as he said to
himself. And when he had decided this he became still
more restless. When talking to the village Elder, the
peasants, or the carpenters, he involuntarily brought the
conversation round to women, and when it turned to
women he kept it on that theme. He noticed the women
more and more.

To settle the matter in his own mind was one thing but to carry it out was another. To approach a woman himself was impossible. Which one? Where? It must be done through someone else, but to whom should he speak about it?

He happened to go into a watchman's hut in the forest to get a drink of water. The watchman had been his father's huntsman, and Yevgeny Ivanovich chatted with him, and the man began telling some strange tales of hunting sprees. It occurred to Yevgeny Ivanovich that it would be convenient to arrange matters in this hut, or in the wood, only he did not know how to manage it and whether old Danila would undertake the arrangement. "Perhaps he will be horrified at such a proposal and I shall have disgraced myself, but perhaps he will agree to it quite simply." So he thought while listening to Danila's stories. Danila was telling how once when they had been stopping at the hut of the sexton's wife in an outlying field, he had brought a woman for Fyodor Zakharich Pryanichnikov.

"It will be all right," thought Yevgeny.

"Your father, may the kingdom of heaven be his, did not go in for nonsense of that kind."

"It won't do," thought Yevgeny. But to test the matter he said: "How was it you engaged on such bad things?"

"But what was there bad in it? She was glad, and Fyodor Zakharich was satisfied, very satisfied. I got a ruble. Why, what was he to do? He too is a lively limb apparently, and drinks wine."

"Yes, I may speak," thought Yevgeny, and at once proceeded to do so.

"And do you know, Danila, I don't know how to endure it." He felt himself going scarlet.

Danila smiled.

"I am not a monk—I have been accustomed to it."

He felt that what he was saying was stupid, but was glad to see that Danila approved.

"Why of course, you should have told me long ago. It can all be arranged," said he: "only tell me which one you want."

"Oh, it is really all the same to me. Of course not an ugly one, and she must be healthy."

"I understand!" said Danila briefly. He reflected.

"Ah! There is a tasty morsel," he began. Again Yevgeny went red. "A tasty morsel. See here, she was married last autumn." Danila whispered—"and he hasn't been able to do anything. Think what that is worth to one who wants it!"

Yevgeny even frowned with shame.

"No, no," he said. "I don't want that at all. I want, on the contrary (what could the contrary be?), on the contrary I only want that she should be healthy and that there should be as little fuss as possible—a woman whose husband is away in the army or something of that kind."

"I know. It's Stepanida I must bring you. Her husband is away in town, just the same as a soldier, and she is a fine woman, and clean. You will be satisfied. As it is I was saying to her the other day—you should go, but she..."

"Well then, when is it to be?"

"Tomorrow if you like. I shall be going to get some tobacco and I will call in, and at the dinner-hour come here, or to the bath-house behind the kitchen garden. There will be nobody about. Besides after dinner everybody takes a nap."

"All right then."

A terrible excitement seized Yevgeny as he rode home. "What will happen? What is a peasant woman like? Suppose it turns out that she is hideous, horrible? No, she is handsome," he told himself, remembering some he had been noticing. "But what shall I say? What shall I do?"

He was not himself all that day. Next day at noon he went to the forester's hut. Danila stood at the door and silently and significantly nodded towards the wood. The blood rushed to Yevgeny's heart, he was conscious of it and went to the kitchen garden. No one was there. He went to the bath-house—there was no one about, he looked in, came out, and suddenly heard the crackling of a breaking twig. He looked round—and she was standing in the thicket beyond the little ravine. He rushed there across the ravine. There were nettles in it which he had not noticed. They stung him and, losing the pince-nez from his nose, he ran up the slope on the farther side. She stood there, in a white embroidered apron, a red-brown skirt, and a bright red kerchief, barefoot, fresh, firm, and handsome, and smiling shyly.

"There is a path leading round—you should have gone round," she said. "I came long ago, ever so long."

He went up to her and, looking her over, touched her.

A quarter of an hour later they separated; he found his pince-nez, called in to see Danila, and in reply to his question: "Are you satisfied, master?" gave him a ruble and went home.

He was satisfied. Only at first had he felt ashamed, then it had passed off. And everything had gone well. The best thing was that he now felt at ease, tranquil and vigorous. As for her, he had not even seen her thoroughly. He remembered that she was clean, fresh, not bad-looking, and simple, without any pretence. "Whose wife is she?" said he to himself. "Pechnikov's, Danila said. What Pechnikov is that? There are two households of that name. Probably she is old Mikhalya's daughter-in-law. Yes, that must be it. His son does live in Moscow. I'll ask Danila about it some time."

From then onward that previously important drawback to country life—enforced self-restraint—was eliminated. Yevgeny's freedom of mind was no longer disturbed and he was able to attend freely to his affairs.

And the matter Yevgeny had undertaken was far

from easy: before he had time to stop up one hole a new one would unexpectedly show itself, and it sometimes seemed to him that he would not be able to go through with it and that it would end in his having to sell the estate after all, which would mean that all his efforts would be wasted and that he had failed to accomplish what he had undertaken. That prospect disturbed him most of all.

All this time more and more debts of his father's unexpectedly came to light. It was evident that towards the end of his life he had borrowed right and left. At the time of the settlement in May, Yevgeny had thought he at least knew everything, but in the middle of the summer he suddenly received a letter from which it appeared that there was still a debt of twelve thousand rubles to the widow Yesipova. There was no promissory note, but only an ordinary receipt which his lawyer told him could be disputed. But it did not enter Yevgeny's head to refuse to pay a debt of his father's merely because the document could be challenged. He only wanted to know for certain whether there had been such a debt.

"Mamma! who is Kaleriya Vladimirovna Yesipova?" he asked his mother when they met as usual for dinner.

"Yesipova? She was brought up by your grandfather. Why?"

Yevgeny told his mother about the letter.

"I wonder she is not ashamed to ask for it. Your father gave her so much!"

"But do we owe her this?"

"Well now, how shall I put it? It is not a debt. Papa, out of his unbounded kindness…"

"Yes, but did Papa consider it a debt?"

"I cannot say. I don't know. I only know it is hard enough for you without that."

Yevgeny saw that Marya Pavlovna did not know what to say, and was as it were sounding him.

"I see from what you say that it must be paid," said he. "I will go to see her tomorrow and have a chat, and see if it cannot be deferred."

"Ah, how sorry I am for you, but you know that will be best. Tell her she must wait," said Marya Pavlovna, evidently tranquillized and proud of her son's decision.

Yevgeny's position was particularly hard because his mother, who was living with him, did not at all realize his position. She had been accustomed all her life long to live so extravagantly that she could not even imagine to herself the position her son was in, that is to say, that today or tomorrow matters might shape themselves so that they would have nothing left and he would have to sell everything and live and support his mother on what salary he could earn, which at the very most would be two thousand rubles. She did not understand that they could only save themselves from that position by cutting down expense in everything, and so she could not understand why Yevgeny was so careful about trifles, in expenditure on gardeners, coachmen, servants—even on food. Also, like most widows, she nourished feelings of devotion to the memory of her departed spouse quite different from those she had felt for him while he lived, and she did not admit the thought that anything the departed had done or arranged could be wrong or could be altered.

Yevgeny by great efforts managed to keep up the garden and the conservatory with two gardeners, and the stables with two coachmen. And Marya Pavlovna naively thought that she was sacrificing herself for her son and doing all a mother could do, by not complaining of the food which the old man-cook prepared, of the fact that the paths in the park were not all swept clean, and that instead of footmen they had only a boy.

So, too, concerning this new debt, in which Yevgeny saw an almost crushing blow to all his undertakings, Marya Pavlovna only saw an incident displaying Yevgeny's noble nature. Moreover she did not feel much anxiety about Yevgeny's position, because she was confident that he would make a brilliant marriage which would put everything right. And he could make a very brilliant marriage: she knew a dozen families who would be glad to give their daughters to him. And she wished to arrange the matter as soon as possible.

IV Yevgeny himself dreamt of marriage, but not in the same way as his mother. The idea of using marriage as a means of putting his affairs in order was repulsive to him. He wished to marry honourably, for love. He observed the girls whom he met and those he knew, and compared himself with them, but no decision had yet been taken. Meanwhile, contrary to his expectations, his relations with Stepanida continued, and even acquired the character of a settled affair. Yevgeny was so far from debauchery, it was so hard for him secretly to do this thing which he felt to be bad, that he could not arrange these meetings himself and even after the first one hoped not to see Stepanida again; but it turned out that after some time the same restlessness (due he believed to that cause) again overcame him. And his restlessness this time was no longer impersonal, but suggested just those same bright, black eyes, and that deep voice, saying, "ever so long," that same scent of something fresh and strong, and that same full breast lifting the bib of her apron, and all this in that hazel and maple thicket, bathed in bright sunlight.

Though he felt ashamed he again approached Danila. And again a rendezvous was fixed for midday in the wood. This time Yevgeny looked her over more carefully and everything about her seemed attractive. He tried talking to her and asked about her husband. He really was Mikhalya's son and lived as a coachman in Moscow.

"Well, then, how is it you…" Yevgeny wanted to ask how it was she was untrue to him.

"What about 'how is it'?" asked she. Evidently she was clever and quick-witted.

"Well, how is it you come to me?"

"There now," said she merrily. "I bet he goes on the spree there. Why shouldn't I?"

Evidently she was putting on an air of sauciness and assurance, and this seemed charming to Yevgeny. But all the same he did not himself fix a rendezvous with her. Even when she proposed that they should meet without the aid of Danila, to whom she seemed not very well disposed, he did not consent. He hoped that this meeting would be the last. He thought such contact was necessary for him and that there was nothing bad about it, but in the depth of his soul there was a stricter judge who did not approve of it and hoped that this would be the last time, or if he did not hope that, at any rate did not wish to participate in arrangements to repeat it another time.

So the whole summer passed, during which they met a dozen times and always by Danila's help. It happened once that she could not be there because her husband had come home, and Danila proposed another woman, but Yevgeny refused with disgust. Then the husband went away and the meetings continued as before, at first through Danila, but afterwards he simply fixed the time and she came with another woman, Prokhorova—as it would not do for a peasant-woman to go about alone.

Once at the very time fixed for the rendezvous a family came to call on Marya Pavlovna, with the very girl she wished Yevgeny to marry, and it was impossible for Yevgeny to get away. As soon as he could do so, he went out as though to the threshing floor, and round by the path to their meeting place in the wood. She was not there, but at the accustomed spot everything within reach had been broken—the black alder, the hazel-twigs, and even a young maple the thickness of a stake. She had waited, had become excited and angry, and had skittishly left him a remembrance. He waited and waited, and then went to Danila to ask him to call her for tomorrow. She came and was just as usual.

So the summer passed. The meetings were always arranged in the wood, and only once, when it grew towards autumn, in the shed that stood in her backyard.

It did not enter Yevgeny's head that these relations of his had any importance for him. About her he did not even think. He gave her money and nothing more. At first he did not know and did not think that the affair was known and that she was envied throughout the village, or that her relations took money from her and encouraged her, and that her conception of any sin in the matter had been quite obliterated by the influence of the money and her family's approval. It seemed to her that if people envied her, then what she was doing was good.

"It is simply necessary for my health," thought

Yevgeny. "I grant it is not right, and though no one says anything, everybody, or many people, know of it. The woman who comes with her knows. And once she knows she is sure to have told others. But what's to be done? I am acting badly," thought Yevgeny, "but what's one to do? Anyhow it is not for long."

What chiefly disturbed Yevgeny was the thought of the husband. At first for some reason it seemed to him that the husband must be a poor sort, and this as it were partly justified his conduct. But he saw the husband and was struck by his appearance: he was a fine fellow and smartly dressed, in no way a worse man than himself, but surely better. At their next meeting he told her he had seen her husband and had been surprised to see that he was such a fine fellow.

"There's not another man like him in the village," said she proudly.

This surprised Yevgeny, and the thought of the husband tormented him still more after that. He happened to be at Danila's one day and Danila, having begun chatting said to him quite openly:

"And Mikhalya asked me the other day: 'Is it true that the master is living with my wife?' I said I did not know. 'Anyway,' I said, 'better with the master than with a peasant.'"

"Well, and what did he say?"

"He said: 'Wait a bit. I'll get to know and I'll give it her all the same.'"

Yes, if the husband returned to live here I would give her up, thought Yevgeny.

But the husband lived in town and for the present their relations continued.

"When necessary I will break it off, and there will be nothing left of it," thought he.

And this seemed to him certain, especially as during the whole summer many different things occupied him very fully: the erection of the new farm-house, and the harvest and building, and above all meeting the debts and selling the wasteland. All these were affairs that completely absorbed him and on which he spent his thoughts when he lay down and when he got up. All that was real life. His relations—he did not even call it connection—with Stepanida he paid no attention to. It is true that when the wish to see her arose it came with such strength that he could think of nothing else. But this did not last long. A meeting was arranged, and he again forgot her for a week or even for a month.

In autumn Yevgeny often rode to town, and there became friendly with the Annenskys. They had a daughter who had just finished the Institute. And then, to Marya Pavlovna's great grief, it happened that Yevgeny "cheapened himself," as she expressed it, by falling in love with Liza Annenskaya and proposing to her.

From that time his relations with Stepanida ceased.

V

It is impossible to explain why Yevgeny chose Liza Annenskaya, as it is always impossible to explain why a man chooses this and not that woman. There were many reasons—positive and negative. One reason was that she was not a very rich heiress such as his mother sought for him, another that she was naive and to be pitied in her relations with her mother, another that she was not a beauty who attracted general attention to herself, and yet she was not bad-looking. But the chief reason was that his acquaintance with her began at the time when he was ripe for marriage. He fell in love because he knew that he would marry.

Liza Annenskaya was at first merely pleasing to Yevgeny, but when he decided to make her his wife his feelings for her became much stronger. He felt that he was in love.

Liza was tall, slender, and long. Everything about her was long; her face, and her nose (not prominently but downwards), and her fingers, and her feet. The colour of her face was very delicate, creamy white and delicately pink; she had long, soft, and curly, light-brown hair, and beautiful eyes, clear, mild, and confiding. Those eyes especially struck Yevgeny, and when he thought of Liza he always saw those clear, mild, confiding eyes.

Such was she physically; he knew nothing of her spiritually, but only saw those eyes. And those eyes seemed to tell him all he needed to know. The meaning of their expression was this:

While still in the Institute, when she was fifteen, Liza used continually to fall in love with all the attractive men she met and was animated and happy only when she was in love. After leaving the Institute she continued to fall in love in just the same way with all the young men she met, and of course fell in love with Yevgeny as soon as she made his acquaintance. It was this being in love which gave her eyes that particular expression which so captivated Yevgeny. Already that winter she had been in love with two young men at one and the same time, and blushed and became excited not only when they entered the room but whenever their names were mentioned. But afterwards, when her mother hinted to her that Irtenev seemed to have serious intentions, her love for him increased so that she became almost indifferent to the two previous attractions, and when Irtenev began to come to their balls and parties and danced with her more than with others and evidently only wished to know whether she loved him, her love for him became painful. She dreamed of him in her sleep and seemed to see him when she was awake in a dark room, and everyone else vanished from her mind. But when he proposed and they were formally engaged, and when they had kissed one another and were a betrothed couple, then she had no thoughts but of him, no desire but to be with him, to love him, and to be loved by him. She was also proud of him and felt emotional about him and herself and her love, and quite melted and felt faint from love of him.

The more he got to know her the more he loved her. He had not at all expected to find such love, and it strengthened his own feeling more.

VI

Towards spring he went to his estate at Semyonovskoe to have a look at it and to give directions about the management, and especially about the house which was being done up for his wedding.

Marya Pavlovna was dissatisfied with her son's choice, not only because the match was not as brilliant as it might have been, but also because she did not like Varvara Alexeevna, his future mother-in-law. Whether she was good-natured or not she did not know and could not decide, but that she was not well-bred, not *comme il faut*—"not a lady" as Marya Pavlovna said to herself— she saw from their first acquaintance, and this distressed her; distressed her because she was accustomed to value breeding and knew that Yevgeny was sensitive to it, and she foresaw that he would suffer much annoyance on this account. But she liked the girl. Liked her chiefly because Yevgeny did. One could not help loving her, and Marya Pavlovna was quite sincerely ready to do so.

Yevgeny found his mother contented and in good spirits. She was getting everything straight in the house and preparing to go away herself as soon as he brought his young wife. Yevgeny persuaded her to stay for the time being, and the future remained undecided.

In the evening after tea Marya Pavlovna played patience as usual. Yevgeny sat by, helping her. This was the hour of their most intimate talks. Having finished one game and while preparing to begin another, she looked up at him and, with a little hesitation, began thus:

"I wanted to tell you, Zhenya—of course I do not know, but in general I wanted to suggest to you—that before your wedding it is absolutely necessary to have finished with all your bachelor affairs so that nothing may disturb either you or your wife. God forbid that it should. You understand me?"

And indeed Yevgeny at once understood that Marya Pavlovna was hinting at his relations with Stepanida which had ended in the previous autumn, and that she attributed much more importance to those relations than they deserved, as solitary women always do. Yevgeny blushed, not from shame so much as from vexation that good-natured Marya Pavlovna was bothering—out of affection no doubt, but still was bothering—about matters that were not her business and that she did not and could not understand. He answered that there was nothing that needed concealment, and that he had always conducted himself so that there should be nothing to hinder his marrying.

"Well, dear, that is excellent. Only, Zhenya... don't be vexed with me," said Marya Pavlovna, and broke off in confusion.

Yevgeny saw that she had not finished and had not said what she wanted to. And this was confirmed, when a little later she began to tell him how, in his absence, she had been asked to stand godmother at ... the Pechnikovs.

Yevgeny flushed again, not with vexation or shame

this time, but with some strange consciousness of the importance of what was about to be told him—an involuntary consciousness quite at variance with his conclusions. And what he expected happened. Marya Pavlovna, as if merely by way of conversation, mentioned that this year only boys were being born—evidently a sign of a coming war. Both at the Vasins and the Pechnikovs the young wife had a first child—at each house a boy. Marya Pavlovna wanted to say this casually, but she herself felt ashamed when she saw the colour mount to her son's face and saw him nervously removing, tapping, and replacing his pince-nez and hurriedly lighting a cigarette. She became silent. He too was silent and could not think how to break that silence. So they both understood that they had understood one another.

"Yes, the chief thing is that there should be justice and no favouritism in the village—as under your grandfather."

"Mamma," said Yevgeny suddenly, "I know why you are saying this. You have no need to be disturbed. My future family life is so sacred to me that I should not infringe it in any case. And as to what occurred in my bachelor days, that is quite ended. I never formed any union and no one has any claims on me."

"Well, I am glad," said his mother. "I know how noble your feelings are."

Yevgeny accepted his mother's words as a tribute due to him, and did not reply.

Next day he drove to town thinking of his fiancée and of anything in the world except of Stepanida. But, as if purposely to remind him, on approaching the church he met people walking and driving back from it. He met old Matvey with Simyon, some lads and girls, and then two women, one elderly, the other, who seemed familiar, smartly dressed and wearing a bright-red kerchief. This woman was walking lightly and boldly, carrying a child in her arms. He came up to them, and the elder woman bowed, stopping in the old-fashioned way, but the young woman with the child only bent her head, and from under the kerchief gleamed familiar, merry, smiling eyes.

Yes, this was she, but all that was over and it was no use looking at her: "and the child may be mine," flashed through his mind. No, what nonsense! There was her husband, she used to see him. He did not even consider the matter further, so settled in his mind was it that it had been necessary for his health—he had paid her money and there was no more to be said; there was, there had been, and there could be, no question of any union between them. It was not that he stifled the voice of conscience, no—his conscience simply said nothing to him. And he thought no more about her after the conversation with his mother and this meeting. Nor did he meet her again.

Yevgeny was married in town the week after Easter, and left at once with his young wife for his country estate. The house had been arranged as usual for a young couple. Marya Pavlovna wished to leave, but Yevgeny begged her to remain, and Liza still more strongly, and she only moved into a detached wing of the house.

And so a new life began for Yevgeny.

VII

The first year of his marriage was a hard one for Yevgeny. It was hard because affairs he had managed to put off during the time of his courtship now, after his marriage, all came upon him at once.

To escape from debts was impossible. An outlying part of the estate was sold and the most pressing obligations met, but others remained, and he had no money. The estate yielded a good revenue, but he had had to send payments to his brother and to spend on his own marriage, so that there was no ready money and the factory could not carry on and would have to be closed down. The only way of escape was to use his wife's money; and Liza, having realized her husband's position, insisted on this herself. Yevgeny agreed, but only on condition that he should give her a mortgage on half his estate, which he did. Of course this was done not for his wife's sake, who felt offended at it, but to appease his mother-in-law.

These affairs with various fluctuations of success and failure helped to poison Yevgeny's life that first year. Another thing was his wife's ill-health. That same first year, seven months after their marriage, a misfortune befell Liza. She was driving out to meet her husband on his return from town, and the quiet horse became rather playful and she was frightened and jumped out. Her jump was comparatively fortunate—she might have been caught by the wheel—but she was pregnant, and that same night the pains began and she had a miscarriage from which she was long in recovering. The loss of the expected child and his wife's illness, together with the disorder in his affairs, and above all the presence of his mother-in-law, who arrived as soon as Liza fell ill—all this together made the year still harder for Yevgeny.

But notwithstanding these difficult circumstances, towards the end of the first year Yevgeny felt very well. First of all his cherished hope of restoring his fallen fortune and renewing his grandfather's way of life in a new form, was approaching accomplishment, though slowly and with difficulty. There was no longer any question of having to sell the whole estate to meet the debts. The chief estate, though transferred to his wife's name, was saved, and if only the beet crop succeeded and the price kept up, by next year his position of want and stress might be replaced by one of complete prosperity. That was one thing.

Another was that however much he had expected from his wife, he had never expected to find in her what he actually found. He found not what he had expected, but something much better.

Raptures of love—though he tried to produce them—did not take place or were very slight, but he discovered something quite different, namely that he was not merely more cheerful and happier but that it had become easier to live. He did not know why this should be so, but it was.

And it was so because immediately after marriage his wife decided that Yevgeny Irtenev was superior to anyone else in the world: wiser, purer, and nobler than they, and that therefore it was right for everyone to serve him and please him; but that as it was impossible to make everyone do this, she must do it herself to the limit of her strength. And she did; directing all her strength of mind towards learning and guessing what he liked, and then doing just that thing, whatever it was and however difficult it might be.

She had the gift which furnishes the chief delight of a relationship with a loving woman: thanks to her love of her husband she penetrated into his soul. She knew his every state and his every shade of feeling—better it seemed to him than he himself—and she behaved correspondingly and therefore never hurt his feelings, but always lessened his distresses and strengthened his joys. And she understood not only his feelings but also his joys. Things quite foreign to her—concerning the farming, the factory, or the appraisement of others—she immediately understood so that she could not merely converse with him, but could often, as he himself said, be a useful and irreplaceable counselor. She regarded affairs and people and everything in the world only through his eyes. She loved her mother, but having seen that Yevgeny disliked his mother-in-law's interference in their life she immediately took her husband's side, and did so with such decision that he had to restrain her.

Besides all this she had very good taste, much tact, and above all she had repose. All that she did, she did unnoticed; only the results of what she did were observable, namely, that always and in everything there was cleanliness, order, and elegance. Liza had at once understood in what her husband's ideal of life consisted, and she tried to attain, and in the arrangement and order of the house did attain, what he wanted. Children it is true were lacking, but there was hope of that also. In winter she went to Petersburg to see a specialist and he assured them that she was quite well and could have children.

And this desire was accomplished. By the end of the year she was again pregnant.

The one thing that threatened, not to say poisoned, their happiness was her jealousy—a jealousy she restrained and did not exhibit, but from which she often suffered. Not only might Yevgeny not love any other woman—because there was not a woman on earth worthy of him (as to whether she herself was worthy or not she never asked herself),—but not a single woman might therefore dare to love him.

VIII   This was how they lived: he rose early, as he always had done, and went to see to the farm or the factory where work was going on, or sometimes to the fields. Towards ten o'clock he would come back for his coffee, which they had on the veranda: Marya Pavlovna, an uncle who lived with them, and Liza. After a conversation which was often very animated while they drank their coffee, they dispersed till dinner-time. At two o'clock they dined and then went for a walk or a drive. In the evening when he returned from the office they drank their evening tea and sometimes he read aloud while she worked, or when there were guests they had music or conversation. When he went away on business he wrote to his wife and received letters from her every day. Sometimes she accompanied him, and then they were particularly merry. On his name-day and on hers guests assembled, and it pleased him to see how well she managed to arrange things so that everybody enjoyed coming. He saw and heard that they all admired her—the young, agreeable hostess—and he loved her still more for this.

All went excellently. She bore her pregnancy easily and, though they were afraid, they both began making plans as to how they would bring the child up. The system of education and the arrangements were all decided by Yevgeny, and her only wish was to carry out his desires obediently. Yevgeny on his part read up medical works and intended to bring the child up according to all the precepts of science. She of course agreed to everything and made preparations, making warm and also cool "envelopes," and preparing a cradle. Thus the second year of their marriage arrived and the second spring.

It was just before Trinity Sunday. Liza was in her fifth month, and though careful she was still brisk and active. Both his mother and hers were living in the house, but under the pretext of watching and safeguarding her only upset her by their tiffs. Yevgeny was specially engrossed with a new experiment for the cultivation of sugar-beet on a large scale.

Just before Trinity Liza decided it was necessary to have a thorough house-cleaning as it had not been done since Easter, and she hired two women by the day to help the servants wash the floors and windows, beat the furniture and the carpets, and put covers on them. These women came early in the morning, heated the coppers, and set to work. One of the two was Stepanida, who had just weaned her baby boy and had begged for the job of washing the floors through the office-clerk— whom she now carried on with. She wanted to have a good look at the new mistress. Stepanida was living by herself as formerly, her husband being away, and she was up to tricks as she had formerly been first with old Danila (who had once caught her taking some logs of firewood), afterwards with the master, and now with the young clerk. She was not concerning herself any longer about her master. "He has a wife now," she thought. But it would be good to have a look at the lady and at her establishment: folk said it was well arranged.

Yevgeny had not seen her since he had met her with the child. Having a baby to attend to she had not been going out to work, and he seldom walked through the village. That morning, on the eve of Trinity Sunday, he got up at five o'clock and rode to the fallow land which was to be sprinkled with phosphates, and had left the house before the women were about, and while they were still engaged lighting the copper fires.

He returned to breakfast merry, contented, and hungry; dismounting from his mare at the gate and handing her over to the gardener. Flicking the high grass with his whip and repeating a phrase he had just uttered, as one often does, he walked towards the house. The phrase was: "phosphates justify"—what or to whom, he neither knew nor reflected.

They were beating a carpet on the grass. The furniture had been brought out.

"There now! What a house-cleaning Liza has undertaken!… Phosphates justify…. What a manageress she is! Yes, a manageress," said he to himself, vividly imagining her in her white wrapper and with her smiling joyful face, as it nearly always was when he looked at her. "Yes, I must change my boots, or else 'phosphates justify,' that is, smell of manure, and the manageress in such a condition. Why 'in such a condition'? Because a new little Irtenev is growing there inside her," he thought. "Yes, phosphates justify," and smiling at his thoughts he put his hand to the door of his room.

But he had not time to push the door before it opened of itself and he came face to face with a woman coming towards him carrying a pail, barefoot and with sleeves turned up high. He stepped aside to let her pass and she too stepped aside, adjusting her kerchief with a wet hand.

"Go on, go on, I won't go in, if you…" began Yevgeny and suddenly stopped, recognizing her.

She glanced merrily at him with smiling eyes, and pulling down her skirt went out the door.

"What nonsense! … It is impossible," said Yevgeny to himself, frowning and waving his hand as though to get rid of a fly, displeased at having noticed her. He was vexed that he had noticed her and yet he could not take his eyes from her strong body, swayed by her agile strides, from her bare feet, or from her arms and shoulders, and the pleasing folds of her shirt and the handsome skirt tucked up high above her white calves.

"But why am I looking?" said he to himself, lowering his eyes so as not to see her. "And anyhow I must go in to get some other boots." And he turned back to go into his own room, but had not gone five steps before he again glanced round to have another look at her without knowing why or wherefore. She was just going round the corner and also glanced at him.

"Ah, what am I doing!" said he to himself. "She may think… It is even certain that she already does think…"

He entered his damp room. Another woman, an old and skinny one, was there, and was still washing it. Yevgeny passed on tiptoe across the floor, wet with dirty water, to the wall where his boots stood, and he was about to leave the room when the woman herself went out.

"This one has gone and the other, Stepanida, will come here alone," someone within him began to reflect.

"My God, what am I thinking of and what am I doing!" He seized his boots and ran out with them into the hall, put them on there, brushed himself, and went out onto the veranda where both the mammas were already drinking coffee. Liza had evidently been expecting him and came onto the veranda through another door at the same time.

My God! If she, who considers me so honourable, pure, and innocent—if she only knew! thought he.

Liza as usual met him with shining face. But today somehow she seemed to him particularly pale, yellow, long, and weak.

X During coffee, as often happened, a peculiarly femi-
nine kind of conversation went on which had no logical
sequence but which evidently was connected in some
way for it went on uninterruptedly.

The two old ladies were pin-pricking one another,
and Liza was skillfully maneuvering between them.

"I am so vexed that we had not finished washing
your room before you got back," she said to her husband.
"But I do so want to get everything arranged."

"Well, did you sleep well after I got up?"

"Yes, I slept well and I feel well."

"How can a woman be well in her condition during
this intolerable heat, when her windows face the sun,"
said Varvara Alexeevna, her mother. "And they have no
venetian-blinds or awnings. I always had awnings."

"But you know we are in the shade after ten o'clock,"
said Marya Pavlovna.

"That's what causes fever; it comes of dampness,"
said Varvara Alexeevna, not noticing that what she was
saying did not agree with what she had just said. "My
doctor always says that it is impossible to diagnose an
illness unless one knows the patient. And he certainly
knows, for he is the leading physician and we pay him a
hundred rubles a visit. My late husband did not believe
in doctors, but he did not grudge me anything."

"How can a man grudge anything to a woman when
perhaps her life and the child's depend…"

"Yes, when she has means a wife need not depend

on her husband. A good wife submits to her husband," said Varvara Alexeevna, "only Liza is too weak after her illness."

"Oh no, mamma, I feel quite well. But why have they not brought you any boiled cream?"

"I don't want any. I can do with raw cream."

"I offered some to Varvara Alexeevna, but she declined," said Marya Pavlovna, as if justifying herself.

"No, I don't want any today." And as if to terminate an unpleasant conversation and yield magnanimously, Varvara Alexeevna turned to Yevgeny and said: "Well, and have you sprinkled the phosphates?"

Liza ran to fetch the cream.

"But I don't want it. I don't want it."

"Liza, Liza, go gently," said Marya Pavlovna. "Such rapid movements do her harm."

"Nothing does harm if one's mind is at peace," said Varvara Alexeevna as if referring to something, though she knew that there was nothing her words could refer to.

Liza returned with the cream and Yevgeny drank his coffee and listened morosely. He was accustomed to these conversations, but today he was particularly annoyed by its lack of sense. He wanted to think over what had happened to him but this chatter disturbed him. Having finished her coffee Varvara Alexeevna went away in a bad humour. Liza, Yevgeny, and Marya Pavlovna stayed behind, and their conversation was simple and pleasant. But Liza, being sensitive, at once noticed that something was tormenting Yevgeny, and she asked him whether anything unpleasant had happened. He was not prepared for this question and hesitated a little before replying that there had been nothing. This reply made Liza think all the more. That something was tormenting him, and greatly tormenting, was as evident to her as that a fly had fallen into the milk, yet he would not speak of it. What could it be?

XI

After breakfast they all dispersed. Yevgeny as usual went to his study, but instead of beginning to read or write his letters, he sat smoking one cigarette after another and thinking. He was terribly surprised and disturbed by the unexpected recrudescence within him of the bad feeling from which he had thought himself free since his marriage. Since then he had not once experienced that feeling, either for her—the woman he had known—or for any other woman except his wife. He had often felt glad of this emancipation, and now suddenly a chance meeting, seemingly so unimportant, revealed to him the fact that he was not free. What now tormented him was not that he was yielding to that feeling and desired her—he did not dream of so doing—but that the feeling was awake within him and he had to be on his guard against it. He had no doubt but that he would suppress it.

He had a letter to answer and a paper to write, and sat down at his writing table and began to work. Having finished it and quite forgotten what had disturbed him, he went out to go to the stables. And again as ill-luck would have it, either by unfortunate chance or intentionally, as soon as he stepped from the porch a red skirt and a red kerchief appeared from round the corner, and she went past him swinging her arms and swaying her body. She not only went past him, but on passing him ran, as if playfully, to overtake her fellow-servant.

Again the bright midday, the nettles, the back of Danila's hut, and in the shade of the plant-trees her smiling face biting some leaves, rose in his imagination.

"No, it is impossible to let matters continue so," he said to himself, and waiting till the women had passed out of sight he went to the office.

It was just the dinner-hour and he hoped to find the steward still there, and so it happened. The steward was just waking up from his after-dinner nap, and stretching himself and yawning was standing in the office, looking at the herdsman who was telling him something.

"Vasily Nikolaevich!" said Yevgeny to the steward.

"What is your pleasure?"

"Just finish what you are saying."

"Aren't you going to bring it in?" said Vasily Nikolaevich to the herdsman.

"It's heavy, Vasily Nikolaevich."

"What is it?" asked Yevgeny.

"Why, a cow has calved in the meadow. Well, all right, I'll order them to harness a horse at once. Tell Nikolay Lysukh to get out the dray cart."

The herdsman went out.

"Do you know," began Yevgeny, flushing and conscious that he was doing so, "do you know, Vasily Nikolaevich, while I was a bachelor I went off the track a bit.... You may have heard…"

Vasily Nikolaevich, evidently sorry for his master, said with smiling eyes: "Is it about Stepanida?"

"Why, yes. Look here. Please, please do not engage

her to help in the house. You understand, it is very awkward for me…"

"Yes, it must have been Vanya the clerk who arranged it."

"Yes, please… and hadn't the rest of the phosphate better be strewn?" said Yevgeny, to hide his confusion.

"Yes, I am just going to see to it."

So the matter ended, and Yevgeny calmed down, hoping that as he had lived for a year without seeing her, so things would go on now. "Besides, Vasily Nikolaevich will speak to Ivan the clerk; Ivan will speak to her, and she will understand that I don't want it," said Yevgeny to himself, and he was glad he had forced himself to speak to Vasily Nikolaevich, hard as it had been to do so.

"Yes, it is better, much better, than that feeling of doubt, that feeling of shame." He shuddered at the mere remembrance of his sin in thought.

XII

The moral effort he had made to overcome his shame and speak to Vasily Nikolaevich tranquillized Yevgeny. It seemed to him that the matter was all over now. Liza at once noticed that he was quite calm, and even happier than usual. "No doubt he was upset by our mothers pin-pricking one another. It really is disagreeable, especially for him who is so sensitive and noble, always to hear such unfriendly and ill-mannered insinuations," thought she.

The next day was Trinity Sunday. It was a beautiful day, and the peasant-women, on their way into the woods to plait wreaths, came, according to custom, to the landowner's home and began to sing and dance. Marya Pavlovna and Varvara Alexeevna came out onto the porch in smart clothes, carrying sunshades, and went up to the ring of singers. With them, in a jacket of Chinese silk, came out the uncle, a flabby libertine and drunkard, who was living that summer with Yevgeny.

As usual there was a bright, many-coloured ring of young women and girls, the centre of everything, and around these from different sides like attendant planets that had detached themselves and were circling round, went girls hand in hand, rustling in their new print gowns; young lads giggling and running backwards and forwards after one another; full-grown lads in dark blue or black coats and caps and with red shirts, who unceasingly spat out sunflower-seed shells; and the domestic servants or other outsiders watching the dance-circle from aside. Both the old ladies went close up to the ring, and Liza accompanied them in a light blue dress, with light blue ribbons on her head, and with wide sleeves under which her long white arms and angular elbows were visible.

Yevgeny did not wish to come out, but it was ridiculous to hide, and he too came out onto the porch smoking a cigarette, bowed to the men and lads, and talked with one of them. The women meanwhile shouted a dance-song with all their might, snapping their fingers, clapping their hands, and dancing.

"They are calling for the master," said a youngster coming up to Yevgeny's wife, who had not noticed the call. Liza called Yevgeny to look at the dance and at one of the women dancers who particularly pleased her. This was Stepanida. She wore a yellow skirt, a velveteen sleeveless jacket and a silk kerchief, and was broad, energetic, ruddy, and merry. No doubt she danced well. He saw nothing.

"Yes, yes," he said, removing and replacing his pincenez. "Yes, yes," he repeated. "So it seems I cannot be rid of her," he thought.

He did not look at her, fearing her attraction, and just on that account what his passing glance caught of her seemed to him especially attractive. Besides this he saw by her sparkling look that she saw him and saw that he admired her. He stood there as long as propriety demanded, and seeing that Varvara Alexeevna had called her "my dear" senselessly and insincerely and was talking to her, he turned aside and went away.

He went into the house in order not to see her, but on reaching the upper story he approached the window, without knowing how or why, and as long as the women remained at the porch he stood there and looked and looked at her, feasting his eyes on her.

He ran, while there was no one to see him, and then went with quiet steps onto the veranda and from there, smoking a cigarette, he passed through the garden as if going for a stroll, and followed the direction she had taken. He had not gone two steps along the alley before he noticed behind the trees a velveteen sleeveless jacket, with a pink and yellow skirt and a red kerchief. She was going somewhere with another woman. "Where are they going?"

And suddenly a terrible desire scorched him as though a hand were seizing his heart. As if by someone else's wish he looked round and went towards her.

"Yevgeny Ivanovich, Yevgeny Ivanovich! I have come to see your honour," said a voice behind him, and Yevgeny, seeing old Samokhin who was digging a well for him, roused himself and turning quickly round went to meet Samokhin. While speaking with him he turned sideways and saw that she and the woman who was with her went down the slope, evidently to the well or making an excuse of the well, and having stopped there a little while ran back to the dance-circle.

XIII After talking to Samokhin, Yevgeny returned to the house as depressed as if he had committed a crime. In the first place she had understood him, believed that he wanted to see her, and desired it herself. Secondly that other woman, Anna Prokhorova, evidently knew of it.

Above all he felt that he was conquered, that he was not master of his own will but that there was another power moving him, that he had been saved only by good fortune, and that if not today then tomorrow or a day later, he would perish all the same.

"Yes, perish," he did not understand it otherwise: to be unfaithful to his young and loving wife with a peasant woman in the village, in the sight of everyone—what was it but to perish, perish utterly, so that it would be impossible to live? No, something must be done.

"My God, my God! What am I to do? Can it be that I shall perish like this?" said he to himself. Is it not possible to do anything? Yet something must be done. Do not think about her," he ordered himself. "Do not think!" and immediately he began thinking and seeing her before him, and seeing also the shade of the plane-tree.

He remembered having read of a hermit who, to avoid the temptation he felt for a woman on whom he had to lay his hand to heal her, thrust his other hand into a brazier and burnt his fingers. He called that to mind. "Yes, I am ready to burn my fingers rather than to perish." He looked round to make sure that there was no one in the room, lit a candle, and put a finger into the flame. "There, now think about her," he said to himself ironically. It hurt him and he withdrew his smoke-stained finger, threw away the match, and laughed at himself. What nonsense! That was not what had to be done. But it was necessary to do something, to avoid seeing her—either to go away himself or to send her away. Yes—send her away. Offer her husband money to remove to town or to another village. People would hear of it and would talk about it. Well, what of that? At any rate it was better than this danger. "Yes, that must be done," he said to himself, and at that very moment he was looking at her without moving his eyes. "Where is she going?" he suddenly asked himself. She, it seemed to him, had seen him at the window and now, having glanced at him and taken another woman by the hand, was going towards the garden swinging her arm briskly. Without knowing why or wherefore, merely in accord with what he had been thinking, he went to the office.

Vasily Nikolaevich in holiday costume and with oiled hair was sitting at tea with his wife and a guest who was wearing an oriental kerchief.

"I want a word with you, Vasily Nikolaevich!"

"Please say what you want to. We have finished tea."

"No. I'd rather you came out with me."

"Directly; only let me get my cap. Tanya, put out the samovar," said Vasily Nikolaevich, stepping outside cheerfully. It seemed to Yevgeny that Vasily had been drinking, but what was to be done? It might be all the better—he would sympathize with him in his difficulties the more readily.

"I have come again to speak about that same matter, Vasily Nikolaevich," said Yevgeny, "about that woman."

"Well, what of her? I told them not to take her again on any account."

"No, I have been thinking in general, and this is what I wanted to take your advice about. Isn't it possible to get them away, to send the whole family away?"

"Where can they be sent?" said Vasily, disapprovingly and ironically as it seemed to Yevgeny.

"Well, I thought of giving them money, or even some land in Koltovsky—so that she should not be here."

"But how can they be sent away? Where is he to go—torn up from his roots? And why should you do it? What harm can she do you?"

"Ah, Vasily Nikolaevich, you must understand that it would be dreadful for my wife to hear of it."

"But who will tell her?"

"How can I live with this dread? The whole thing is very painful for me."

"But really, why should you distress yourself? Whoever stirs up the past—out with his eye! Who is not a sinner before God and to blame before the Tsar, as the saying is?"

"All the same it would be better to get rid of them. Can't you speak to the husband?"

"But it is no use speaking! Eh, Yevgeny Ivanovich,

what is the matter with you? It is all past and forgotten. All sorts of things happen. Who is there that would now say anything bad of you? Everybody sees you."

"But all the same go and have a talk with him."

"All right, I will speak to him."

Though he knew that nothing would come of it, this talk somewhat calmed Yevgeny. Above all, it made him feel that through excitement he had been exaggerating the danger.

Had he gone to meet her by appointment? It was impossible. He had simply gone to stroll in the garden and she had happened to run out at the same time.

XIV After dinner that very Trinity Sunday Liza while walking from the garden to the meadow, where her husband wanted to show her the clover, took a false step and fell when crossing a little ditch. She fell gently, on her side; but she gave an exclamation, and her husband saw an expression in her face not only of fear but of pain. He was about to help her up, but she motioned him away with her hand.

"No, wait a bit, Yevgeny," she said, with a weak smile, and looked up guiltily as it seemed to him. "My foot only gave way under me."

"There, I always say," remarked Varvara Alexeevna, "can anyone in her condition possibly jump over ditches?"

"But it is all right, mamma. I shall get up directly." With her husband's help she did get up, but she immediately turned pale, and looked frightened.

"Yes, I am not well!" and she whispered something to her mother.

"Oh, my God, what have you done! I said you ought not to go there," cried Varvara Alexeevna. "Wait—I will call the servants. She must not walk. She must be carried!"

"Don't be afraid, Liza, I will carry you," said Yevgeny, putting his left arm round her. "Hold me by the neck. Like that." And stopping down he put his right arm under her knees and lifted her. He could never afterwards forget the suffering and yet beatific expression of her face.

"I am too heavy for you, dear," she said with a smile. "Mamma is running, tell her!" And she bent towards him and kissed him. She evidently wanted her mother to see how he was carrying her.

Yevgeny shouted to Varvara Alexeevna not to hurry, and that he would carry Liza home. Varvara Alexeevna stopped and began to shout still louder.

"You will drop her, you'll be sure to drop her. You want to destroy her. You have no conscience!"

"But I am carrying her excellently."

"I do not want to watch you killing my daughter, and I can't." And she ran round the bend in the alley.

"Never mind, it will pass," said Liza, smiling.

"Yes, if only it does not have consequences like last time."

"No. I am not speaking of that. That is all right. I mean mamma. You are tired. Rest a bit."

But though he found it heavy, Yevgeny carried his burden proudly and gladly to the house and did not hand her over to the housemaid and the man-cook whom Varvara Alexeevna had found and sent to meet them. He carried her to the bedroom and put her on the bed.

"Now go away," she said, and drawing his hand to her she kissed it. "Annushka and I will manage all right."

Marya Pavlovna also ran in from her rooms in the wing. They undressed Liza and laid her on the bed.

Yevgeny sat in the drawing room with a book in his hand, waiting. Varvara Alexeevna went past him with such a reproachfully gloomy air that he felt alarmed.

"Well, how is it?" he asked.

"How is it? What's the good of asking? It is probably what you wanted when you made your wife jump over the ditch."

"Varvara Alexeevna!" he cried. "This is impossible. If you want to torment people and to poison their life" —he wanted to say— "then go elsewhere to do it," but restrained himself. "How is it that it does not hurt you?"

"It is too late now." And shaking her cap in a triumphant manner she passed out by the door.

The fall had really been a bad one; Liza's foot had twisted awkwardly and there was danger of her having another miscarriage. Everyone knew that there was nothing to be done but that she must just lie quietly, yet all the same they decided to send for a doctor.

"Dear Nikolay Semyonich," wrote Yevgeny to the doctor, "you have always been so kind to us that I hope you will not refuse to come to my wife's assistance. She…" and so on. Having written the letter he went to the stables to arrange about the horses and the carriage. Horses had to be got ready to bring the doctor and others to take him back. When an estate is not run on a large scale, such things cannot be quickly decided but have to be considered. Having arranged it all and dispatched the coachman, it was past nine before he got back to the house. His wife was lying down, and said that she felt perfectly well and had no pain. But Varvara Alexeevna was sitting with a lamp screened from Liza by some sheets of music and knitting a large red coverlet, with a mien that said that after what had happened peace was impossible, but that she at any rate would do her duty no matter what anyone else did.

Yevgeny noticed this, but, to appear as if he had not done so, tried to assume a cheerful and tranquil air and told how he had chosen the horses and how capitally the mare, Kabushka, had galloped as left trace-horse in the troika.

"Yes, of course, it is just the time to exercise the horses when help is needed. Probably the doctor will also be thrown into the ditch," remarked Varvara Alexeevna, examining her knitting from under her pince-nez and moving it close up to the lamp.

"But you know we had to send one way or another, and I made the best arrangement I could."

"Yes, I remember very well how your horses galloped with me under the arch of the gateway." This was a long-standing fancy of hers, and Yevgeny now was injudicious enough to remark that that was not quite what had happened.

"It is not for nothing that I have always said, and have often remarked to the prince, that it is hardest of all to live with people who are untruthful and insincere. I can endure anything except that."

"Well, if anyone has to suffer more than another, it is certainly I," said Yevgeny. "But you…"

"Yes, it is evident."

"What?"

"Nothing, I am only counting my stitches."

Yevgeny was standing at the time by the bed and Liza was looking at him, and one of her moist hands outside the coverlet caught his hand and pressed it. "Bear with her for my sake. You know she cannot prevent our loving one another," was what her look said.

"I won't do so again. It's nothing," he whispered, and he kissed her damp, long hand and then her affectionate eyes, which closed while he kissed them.

"Can it be the same thing over again?" he asked. "How are you feeling?"

"I am afraid to say for fear of being mistaken, but I feel that he is alive and will live," said she, glancing at her stomach.

"Ah, it is dreadful, dreadful to think of."

Notwithstanding Liza's insistence that he should go away, Yevgeny spent the night with her, hardly closing an eye and ready to attend on her.

But she passed the night well, and had they not sent for the doctor she would perhaps have got up.

By dinner-time the doctor arrived and of course said that though if the symptoms recurred there might be cause for apprehension, yet actually there were no positive symptoms, but as there were also no contrary

indications one might suppose on the one hand that—
and on the other hand that... And therefore she must
lie still, and that "though I do not like prescribing, yet
all the same she should take this mixture and should lie
quiet." Besides this, the doctor gave Varvara Alexeevna
a lecture on woman's anatomy, during which Varvara
Alexeevna nodded her head significantly. Having
received his fee, as usual into the backmost part of his
palm, the doctor drove away and the patient was left to
lie in bed for a week.

XV

Yevgeny spent most of his time by his wife's bedside, talking to her, reading to her, and what was hardest of all, enduring without murmur Varvara Alexeevna's attacks, and even contriving to turn these into jokes.

But he could not stay at home all the time. In the first place his wife sent him away, saying that he would fall ill if he always remained with her; and secondly the farming was progressing in a way that demanded his presence at every step. He could not stay at home, but had to be in the fields, in the wood, in the garden, at the threshing-floor; and everywhere he was pursued not merely by the thought but by the vivid image of Stepanida, and he only occasionally forgot her. But that would not have mattered, he could perhaps have mastered his feeling; what was worst of all was that, whereas he had previously lived for months without seeing her, he now continually came across her. She evidently understood that he wished to renew relations with her and tried to come in his way. Nothing was said either by him or by her, and therefore neither he nor she went directly to a rendezvous, but only sought opportunities of meeting.

The most possible place for them to meet was in the forest, where peasant-women went with sacks to collect grass for their cows. Yevgeny knew this and therefore went there every day. Every day he told himself that he would not go, and every day it ended by his making his way to the forest and, on hearing the sound of voices, standing behind the bushes with sinking heart looking to see if she was there.

Why he wanted to know whether it was she who was there, he did not know. If it had been she and she had been alone, he would not have gone to her—so he believed—he would have run away; but he wanted to see her.

Once he met her. As he was entering the forest she came out of it with two other women, carrying a heavy sack full of grass on her back. A little earlier he would perhaps have met her in the forest. Now, with the other women there, she could not go back to him. But though he realized this impossibility, he stood for a long time behind a hazel bush, at the risk of attracting the other women's attention. Of course she did not return, but he stayed there a long time and, great heavens, how delightful his imagination made her appear to him! And this not only once, but five or six times, and each time more intensely. Never had she seemed so attractive, and never had he been so completely in her power.

He felt that he had lost control of himself and had become almost insane. His strictness with himself had not weakened a jog; on the contrary he saw all the abomination of his desire and even of his action, for his going to the wood was an action. He knew that he only need come near her anywhere in the dark, and if possible touch her, and he would yield to his feelings. He knew that it was only shame before people, before her, and no doubt before himself that restrained him. And he knew too that he had sought conditions in which that shame would not be apparent—darkness or proximity—in which it would be stifled by animal passion. And therefore he knew that he was a wretched criminal, and despised and hated himself with all his soul. He hated himself because he still had not surrendered: every day he prayed God to strengthen him, to save him from perishing; every day he determined that from today onward he would not take a step to see her, and would forget her. Every day he devised means of delivering himself from this enticement, and he made use of those means.

But it was all in vain.

One of the means was continual occupation; another was intense physical work and fasting; a third was imagining to himself the shame that would fall upon him when everybody knew of it—his wife, his mother-in-law, and the folk around. He did all this and it seemed to him that he was conquering, but midday came—the hour of their former meetings and the hour when he had met her carrying the grass—and he went to the forest. Thus five days of torment passed. He only saw her from a distance, and did not once encounter her.

XVI

Liza was gradually recovering, she could move about and was only uneasy at the change that had taken place in her husband, which she did not understand.

Varvara Alexeevna had gone away for a while, and the only visitor was Yevgeny's uncle. Marya Pavlovna was as usual at home.

Yevgeny was in his semi-insane condition when there came two days of pouring rain, as often happens after thunder in June. The rain stopped all work. They even ceased carting manure on account of the dampness and dirt. The peasants remained at home. The herdsmen wore themselves out with the cattle, and eventually drove them home. The cows and sheep wandered about in the pastureland and ran loose in the grounds. The peasant women, barefoot and wrapped in shawls, splashing through the mud, rushed about to seek the runaway cows. Streams flowed everywhere along the paths, all the leaves and all the grass were saturated with water, and streams flowed unceasingly from the spouts into the bubbling puddles. Yevgeny sat at home with his wife, who was particularly wearisome that day. She questioned Yevgeny several times as to the cause of his discontent, and he replied with vexation that nothing was the matter. She ceased questioning him but was still distressed.

They were sitting after breakfast in the drawing room. His uncle for the hundredth time was recounting fabrications about his society acquaintances. Liza was knitting a jacket and sighed, complaining of the weather and of a pain in the small of her back. The uncle advised her to lie down, and asked for vodka for himself. It was terribly dull for Yevgeny in the house. Everything was weak and dull. He read a book and a magazine, but understood nothing of them.

"I must go out and look at the rasping-machine they brought yesterday," said he, and got up and went out.

"Take an umbrella with you."

"Oh, no, I have a leather coat. And I am only going as far as the boiling-room."

He put on his boots and his leather coat and went to the factory; and he had not gone twenty steps before he met her coming towards him, with her skirts tucked up high above her white calves. She was walking, holding down the shawl in which her head and shoulders were wrapped.

"Where are you going?" said he, not recognizing her the first instant. When he recognized her it was already too late. She stopped, smiling, and looked long at him.

"I am looking for a calf. Where are you off to in such weather?" said she, as if she were seeing him every day.

"Come to the shed," said he suddenly, without knowing how he said it. It was as if someone else had uttered the words.

She bit her shawl, winked, and ran in the direction which led from the garden to the shed, and he continued his path, intending to turn off beyond the lilac-bush and go there too.

"Master," he heard a voice behind him. "The mistress is calling you, and wants you to come back for a minute."

This was Misha, his man-servant.

"My God! This is the second time you have saved me," thought Yevgeny, and immediately turned back. His wife reminded him that he had promised to take some medicine at the dinner hour to a sick woman, and he had better take it with him.

While they were getting the medicine some five minutes elapsed, and then, going away with the medicine, he hesitated to go direct to the shed lest he should be seen from the house, but as soon as he was out of sight he promptly turned and made his way to it. He already saw her in imagination inside the shed smiling gaily. But she was not there, and there was nothing in the shed to show that she had been there.

He was already thinking that she had not come, had not heard or understood his words—he had muttered them through his nose as if afraid of her hearing them— or perhaps she had not wanted to come. "And why did I imagine that she would rush to me? She has her own husband; it is only I who am such a wretch as to have a wife, and a good one, and to run after another." Thus he thought sitting in the shed, the thatch of which had a leak and dripped from its straw. "But how delightful it would be if she did come—alone here in this rain.

If only I could embrace her once again, then let happen what may. But I could tell if she has been here by her footprints," he reflected. He looked at the trodden ground near the shed and at the path overgrown by grass, and the fresh print of bare feet, and even of one that had slipped, was visible.

"Yes, she has been here. Well, now it is settled. Wherever I may see her I shall go straight to her. I will go to her at night." He sat for a long time in the shed and left it exhausted and crushed. He delivered the medicine, returned home, and lay down in his room to wait for dinner.

XVII

Before dinner Liza came to him and, still wondering what could be the cause of his discontent, began to say that she was afraid he did not like the idea of her going to Moscow for her confinement, and that she had decided that she would remain at home and on no account go to Moscow. He knew how she feared both her confinement itself and the risk of not having a healthy child, and therefore he could not help being touched at seeing how ready she was to sacrifice everything for his sake. All was so nice, so pleasant, so clean, in the house; and in his soul it was so dirty, despicable, and foul. The whole evening Yevgeny was tormented by knowing that notwithstanding his sincere repulsion at his own weakness, notwithstanding his firm intention to break off—the same thing would happen again tomorrow.

"No, this is impossible," he said to himself, walking up and down in his room. "There must be some remedy for it. My God! What am I to do?"

Someone knocked at the door as foreigners do. He knew this must be his uncle. "Come in," he said.

The uncle had come as a self-appointed ambassador from Liza.

"Do you know, I really do notice that there is a change in you," he said,—"and Liza—I understand how it troubles her. I understand that it must be hard for you to leave all the business you have so excellently started, but *que veux-tu*? I should advise you to go away. it will be more satisfactory both for you and for her. And do you know, I should advise you to go to the Crimea. The climate is beautiful and there is an excellent midwife there, and you would be just in time for the best of the grape season."

"Uncle," Yevgeny suddenly exclaimed. "Can you keep a secret? A secret that is terrible to me, a shameful secret."

"Oh, come—do you really feel any doubt of me?"

"Uncle, you can help me. Not only help, but save me!" said Yevgeny. And the thought of disclosing his secret to his uncle whom he did not respect, the thought that he should show himself in the worst light and humiliate himself before him, was pleasant. He felt himself to be despicable and guilty, and wished to punish himself.

"Speak, my dear fellow, you know how fond I am of you," said the uncle, evidently well content that there was a secret and that it was a shameful one, and that it would be communicated to him, and that he could be of use.

"First of all I must tell you that I am a wretch, a good-for-nothing, a scoundrel—a real scoundrel."

"Now what are you saying…" began his uncle, as if he were offended.

"What! Not a wretch when I—Liza's husband, Liza's! One has only to know her purity, her love—and that I, her husband, want to be untrue to her with a peasant-woman!"

"What is this? Why do you want to—you have not been unfaithful to her?"

"Yes, at least just the same as being untrue, for it did not depend on me. I was ready to do so. I was hindered, or else I should… now. I do not know what I should have done…"

"But please, explain to me…"

"Well, it is like this. When I was a bachelor I was stupid enough to have relations with a woman here in our village. That is to say, I used to have meetings with her in the forest, in the field…"

"Was she pretty?" asked his uncle.

Yevgeny frowned at this question, but he was in such need of external help that he made as if he did not hear it, and continued:

"Well, I thought this was just casual and that I should break it off and have done with it. And I did break it off before my marriage. For nearly a year I did not see her or think about her." It seemed strange to Yevgeny himself to hear the description of his own condition. "Then suddenly, I don't myself know why—really one sometimes believes in witchcraft—I saw her, and a worm crept into my heart; and it gnaws. I reproach myself, I understand the full horror of my action, that is to say, of the act I may commit any moment, and yet I myself turn to it, and if I have not committed it, it is only because God preserved me. Yesterday I was on my way to see her when Liza sent for me."

"What, in the rain?"

"Yes. I am worn out, Uncle, and have decided to

confess to you and to ask your help."

"Yes, of course, it's a bad thing on your own estate. People will get to know. I understand that Liza is weak and that it is necessary to spare her, but why on your own estate?"

Again Yevgeny tried not to hear what his uncle was saying, and hurried on to the core of the matter.

"Yes, save me from myself. That is what I ask of you. Today I was hindered by chance. But tomorrow or next time no one will hinder me. And she knows now. Don't leave me alone."

"Yes, all right," said his uncle,—" but are you really so much in love?"

"Oh, it is not that at all. It is not that, it is some kind of power that has seized me and holds me. I do not know what to do. Perhaps I shall gain strength, and then…"

"Well, it turns out as I suggested," said his uncle. "Let us be off to the Crimea."

"Yes, yes, let us go, and meanwhile you will be with me and will talk to me."

The fact that Yevgeny had confided his secret to his uncle, and still more the sufferings of his conscience and the feeling of shame he experienced after that rainy day, sobered him. It was settled that they would start for Yalta in a week's time. During that week Yevgeny drove to town to get money for the journey, gave instructions from the house and from the office concerning the management of the estate, again became gay and friendly with his wife, and began to awaken morally.

So without having once seen Stepanida after that rainy day he left with his wife for the Crimea. There he spent an excellent two months. He received so many new impressions that it seemed to him that the past was obliterated from his memory. In the Crimea they met former acquaintances and became particularly friendly with them, and they also made new acquaintances. Life in the Crimea was a continual holiday for Yevgeny, besides being instructive and beneficial. They became friendly there with the former marshal of the nobility of their province, a clever and liberal-minded man who became fond of Yevgeny and coached him, and attracted him to his party.

At the end of August Liza gave birth to a beautiful, healthy daughter, and her confinement was unexpectedly easy.

In September they returned home, the four of them, including the baby and its wet-nurse, as Liza was unable to nurse it herself. Yevgeny returned home entirely free from the former horrors and quite a new and happy man. Having gone through all that a husband goes through when his wife bears a child, he loved her more than ever. His feeling for the child when he took it in his arms was a funny, new, very pleasant and, as it were, a tickling feeling. Another new thing in his life now was that, besides his occupation with the estate, thanks to his acquaintance with Dumchin (the ex-marshal) a new interest occupied his mind, that of the *zemstvo*—partly an ambitious interest, partly a feeling of duty. In October there was to be a special Assembly, at which he was to be elected. After arriving home he drove once to town and another time to Dumchin.

Of the torments of his temptation and struggle he had forgotten even to think, and could with difficulty recall them to mind. It seemed to him something like an attack of insanity he had undergone.

To such an extent did he now feel free from it that he was not even afraid to make inquiries on the first occasion when he remained alone with the steward. As he had previously spoken to him about the matter he was not ashamed to ask.

"Well, and is Sidor Pechnikov still away from home?" he inquired.

"Yes, he is still in town."

"And his wife?"

"Oh, she is a worthless woman. She is now carrying on with Zinovey. She has gone quite on the loose."

"Well, that is all right," thought Yevgeny. "How wonderfully indifferent to it I am! How I have changed."

All that Yevgeny had wished had been realized. He had obtained the property, the factory was working successfully, the beet-crops were excellent, and he expected a large income; his wife had borne a child satisfactorily, his mother-in-law had left, and he had been unanimously elected to the *zemstvo*.

He was returning home from town after the election. He had been congratulated and had had to return thanks. He had had dinner and had drunk some five glasses of champagne. Quite new plans of life now presented themselves to him, and he was thinking about these as he drove home. It was the Indian summer: an excellent road and a hot sun. As he approached his home Yevgeny was thinking of how, as a result of this election, he would occupy among the people the position he had always dreamed of; that is to say, one in which he would be able to serve them not only by production, which gave employment, but also by direct influence. He imagined what his own and the other peasants would think of him in three years' time. "For instance this one," he thought, drifting just then through the village and glancing at a peasant who with a peasant woman was crossing the street in front of him carrying a full water-tub. They stopped to let his carriage pass. The peasant was old Pechnikov, and the woman was Stepanida. Yevgeny looked at her, recognized her, and was glad to feel that he remained quite tranquil. She was still as good looking as ever, but this did not touch him at all. He drove home.

"Well, may we congratulate you?" said his uncle.

"Yes, I was elected."

"Capital! We must drink to it!"

Next day Yevgeny drove about to see to the farming which he had been neglecting. At the outlying farmstead a new threshing machine was at work. While watching it Yevgeny stepped among the women, trying not to take notice of them; but try as he would he once or twice noticed the black eyes and red kerchief of Stepanida, who was carrying away the straw. Once or twice he glanced sideways at her and felt that something was happening, but could not account for it to himself. Only next day, when he again drove to the threshing floor and spent two hours there quite unnecessarily, without ceasing to caress with his eyes the familiar, handsome figure of the young woman, did he feel that he was lost, irremediably lost. Again those torments! Again all that horror and fear, and there was no saving himself.

What he expected happened to him. The evening of the next day, without knowing how, he found himself at her back yard, by her hay shed, where in autumn they had once had a meeting. As though having a stroll, he stopped there lighting a cigarette. A neighbouring peasant-woman saw him, and as he turned back he heard her say to someone: "Go, he is waiting for you—on my dying word he is standing there. Go, you fool!"

He saw how a woman—she—ran to the hay shed; but as a peasant had met him it was no longer possible for him to turn back, and so he went home.

XX When he entered the drawing-room everything seemed strange and unnatural to him. He had risen that morning vigorous, determined to fling it all aside, to forget it and not allow himself to think about it. But without noticing how it occurred he had all the morning not merely not interested himself in the work, but tried to avoid it. What had formerly cheered him and been important was now insignificant. Unconsciously he tried to free himself from business. It seemed to him that he had to do so in order to think and to plan. And he freed himself and remained alone. But as soon as he was alone he began to wander about in the garden and the forest. And all those spots were besmirched in his recollection by memories that gripped him. He felt that he was walking in the garden and pretending to himself that he was thinking out something, but that really he was not thinking out anything, but insanely and unreasonably expecting her; expecting that by some miracle she would be aware that he was expecting her, and would come here at once and go somewhere where no one would see them, or would come at night when there would be no moon, and no one, not even she herself, would see—on such a night she would come and he would touch her body....

"There now, talking of breaking off when I wish to," he said to himself. "Yes, and that is having a clean healthy woman for one's health sake! No, it seems one can't play with her like that. I thought I had taken her, but it was she who took me; took me and does not let me go. Why, I thought I was free, but I was not free and was deceiving myself when I married. It was all nonsense—fraud. From the time I had her I experienced a new feeling, the real feeling of a husband. Yes, I ought to have lived with her.

"One of two lives is possible for me: that which I began with Liza: service, estate management, the child, and people's respect. If that is life, it is necessary that she, Stepanida, should not be there. She must be sent away, as I said, or destroyed so that she shall not exist. And the other life—is this: For me to take her away from her husband, pay him money, disregard the shame and disgrace, and live with her. But in that case it is necessary that Liza should not exist, nor Mimi (the baby). No, that is not so, the baby does not matter, but it is necessary that there should be no Liza—that she should go away—that she should know, curse me, and go away. That she should know that I have exchanged her for a peasant woman, that I am a deceiver and a scoundrel!— No, that is too terrible! It is impossible. But it might happen," he went on thinking—"it might happen that Liza might fall ill and die. Die, and then everything would be capital.

"Capital! Oh, scoundrel! No, if someone must die it should be Stepanida. If she were to die, how good it would be.

"Yes, that is how men come to poison or kill their

wives or lovers. Take a revolver and go and call her, and instead of embracing her, shoot her in the breast and have done with it.

"Really she is—a devil. Simply a devil. She has possessed herself of me against my own will.

"Kill? Yes. There are only two ways out: to kill my wife or her. For it is impossible to live like this.

[At this place the alternative ending, printed at the end of the story, begins.]

"It is impossible! I must consider the matter and look ahead. If things remain as they are what will happen? I shall again be saying to myself that I do not wish it and that I will throw her off, but it will be merely words; in the evening I shall be at her back yard, and she will know it and will come out. And if people know of it and tell my wife, or if I tell her myself—for I can't lie —I shall not be able to live so. I cannot! People will know. They will all know—Parasha and the blacksmith. Well, is it possible to live so?

"Impossible! There are only two ways out: to kill my wife, or to kill her. yes, or else… Ah, yes, there is a third way: to kill myself," said he softly, and suddenly a shudder ran over his skin. "Yes, kill myself, then I shall not need to kill them." He became frightened, for he felt that only that way was possible. He had a revolver. "Shall I really kill myself? It is something I never thought of— how strange it will be…"

He returned to his study and at once opened the

cupboard where the revolver lay, but before he had taken
it out of its case his wife entered the room.

He threw a newspaper over the revolver.

"Again the same!" said she aghast when she had looked at him.

"What is the same?"

"The same terrible expression that you had before and would not explain to me. Zhenya, dear one, tell me about it. I see that you are suffering. Tell me and you will feel easier. Whatever it may be, it will be better than for you to suffer so. Don't I know that it is nothing bad?"

"You know? While…"

"Tell me, tell me, tell me. I won't let you go."

He smiled a piteous smile.

"Shall I?—No, it is impossible. And there is nothing to tell."

Perhaps he might have told her, but at that moment the wet-nurse entered to ask if she should go for a walk. Liza went out to dress the baby.

"Then you will tell me? I will be back directly."

"Yes, perhaps…"

She never could forget the piteous smile with which he said this. She went out.

Hurriedly, stealthily like a robber, he seized the revolver and took it out of its case. It was loaded, yes, but long ago, and one cartridge was missing.

"Well, how will it be?" He put it to his temple and hesitated a little, but as soon as he remembered Stepanida—his decision not to see her, his struggle, temptation, fall, and renewed struggle—he shuddered with horror. "No, this is better," and he pulled the trigger...

When Liza ran into the room—she had only had time to step down from the balcony—he was lying face downwards on the floor: black, warm blood was gushing from the wound, and his corpse was twitching.

There was an inquest. No one could understand or explain the suicide. It never even entered his uncle's head that its cause could be anything in common with the confession Yevgeny had made to him two months previously.

Varvara Alexeevna assured them that she had always foreseen it. It had been evident from his way of disputing. Neither Liza nor Marya Pavlovna could at all understand why it had happened, but still they did not believe what the doctors said, namely, that he was mentally deranged—a psychopath. They were quite unable to accept this, for they knew he was saner than hundreds of their acquaintances.

And indeed if Yevgeny Irtenev was mentally deranged everyone is in the same case; the most mentally deranged people are certainly those who see in others indications of insanity they do not notice in themselves.

VARIATION OF THE CONCLUSION TO *THE DEVIL*

"To kill, yes. There are only two ways out: to kill my wife, or to kill her. For it is impossible to live like this," said he to himself, and going up to the table he took from it a revolver and, having examined it—one cartridge was wanting—he put it in his trouser pocket.

"My God! What am I doing?" he suddenly exclaimed, and folding his hands he began to pray.

"O God, help me and deliver me! Thou knowest that I do not desire evil, but by myself am powerless. Help me," said he, making the sign of the cross on his breast before the icon.

"Yes, I can control myself. I will go out, walk about and think things over."

He went to the entrance-hall, put on his overcoat and went out onto the porch. Unconsciously his steps took him past the garden along the field path to the outlying farmstead. There the threshing machine was still droning and the cries of the driver lads were heard. He entered the barn. She was there. He saw her at once. She was raking up the corn, and on seeing him she ran briskly and merrily about, with laughing eyes, raking up the scattered corn with agility. Yevgeny could not help watching her though he did not wish to do so. He only recollected himself when she was no longer in sight. The clerk informed him that they were now finishing threshing the corn that had been beaten down—that was why it was going slower and the output was less. Yevgeny went up to the drum, which occasionally gave a knock as sheaves not evenly fed in passed under it, and he asked the clerk if there were many such sheaves of beaten-down corn.

"There will be five cartloads of it."

"Then look here…" began Yevgeny, but he did not finish the sentence. She had gone close up to the drum and was raking the corn from under it, and she scorched him with her laughing eyes. That look spoke of a merry, careless love between them, of the fact that she knew he wanted her and had come to her shed, and that she as always was ready to live and be merry with him regardless of all conditions or consequences. Yevgeny felt himself to be in her power but did not wish to yield.

He remembered his prayer and tried to repeat it. He began saying it to himself, but at once felt that it was useless. A single thought now engrossed him entirely: how to arrange a meeting with her so that the others should not notice it.

"If we finish this lot today, are we to start on a fresh stack or leave it till tomorrow?" asked the clerk.

"Yes, yes," replied Yevgeny, involuntarily following her to the heap to which with the other women she was raking the corn.

"But can I really not master myself?" said he to himself. "Have I really perished? O God! But there is not God. There is only a devil. And it is she. She has possessed me. But I won't, I won't! A devil, yes, a devil."

Again he went up to her, drew the revolver from his

pocket and shot her, once, twice, thrice, in the back. She ran a few steps and fell on the heap of corn.

"My God, my God! What is that?" cried the women.

"No, it was not an accident. I killed her on purpose," cried Yevgeny. "Send for the police officer."

He went home and went to his study and locked himself in, without speaking to his wife.

"Do not come to me," he cried to her through the door. "You will know all about it."

An hour later he rang, and bade the man-servant who answered the bell: "Go and find out whether Stepanida is alive."

The servant already knew all about it, and told him she had died an hour ago.

"Well, all right. Now leave me alone. When the police officer or the magistrate comes, let me know."

The police officer and magistrate arrived next morning, and Yevgeny, having bidden his wife and baby farewell, was taken to prison.

He was tried. It was during the early days of trial by jury, and the verdict was one of temporary insanity, and he was sentenced only to perform church penance.

He had been kept in prison for nine months and was then confined in a monastery for one month.

He had begun to drink while still in prison, continued to do so in the monastery, and returned home an enfeebled, irresponsible drunkard.

Varvara Alexeevna assured them that she had always

predicted this. It was, she said, evident from the way he disputed. Neither Liza nor Marya Pavlovna could understand how the affair had happened, but for all that, they did not believe what the doctors said, namely, that he was mentally deranged—a psychopath. They could not accept that, for they knew that he was saner than hundreds of their acquaintances.

And indeed, if Yevgeny Irtenev was mentally deranged when he committed this crime, then everyone is similarly insane. The most mentally deranged people are certainly those who see in others indications of insanity they do not notice in themselves.

OTHER TITLES IN
THE ART OF THE NOVELLA SERIES

BARTLEBY THE SCRIVENER / HERMAN MELVILLE
THE LESSON OF THE MASTER / HENRY JAMES
MY LIFE / ANTON CHEKHOV
THE DEVIL / LEO TOLSTOY
THE TOUCHSTONE / EDITH WHARTON
THE HOUND OF THE BASKERVILLES / ARTHUR CONAN DOYLE
THE DEAD / JAMES JOYCE
FIRST LOVE / IVAN TURGENEV
A SIMPLE HEART / GUSTAVE FLAUBERT
THE MAN WHO WOULD BE KING / RUDYARD KIPLING
MICHAEL KOHLHAAS / HEINRICH VON KLEIST
THE BEACH OF FALESÁ / ROBERT LOUIS STEVENSON
THE HORLA / GUY DE MAUPASSANT
THE ETERNAL HUSBAND / FYODOR DOSTOEVSKY
THE MAN THAT CORRUPTED HADLEYBURG / MARK TWAIN
THE LIFTED VEIL / GEORGE ELIOT
THE GIRL WITH THE GOLDEN EYES / HONORÉ DE BALZAC
A SLEEP AND A FORGETTING / WILLIAM DEAN HOWELLS
BENITO CERENO / HERMAN MELVILLE
MATHILDA / MARY SHELLEY
STEMPENYU: A JEWISH ROMANCE / SHOLEM ALEICHEM
FREYA OF THE SEVEN ISLES / JOSEPH CONRAD
HOW THE TWO IVANS QUARRELLED / NIKOLAI GOGOL
MAY DAY / F. SCOTT FITZGERALD
RASSELAS, PRINCE ABYSSINIA / SAMUEL JOHNSON
THE DIALOGUE OF THE DOGS / MIGUEL DE CERVANTES
THE LEMOINE AFFAIR / MARCEL PROUST
THE COXON FUND / HENRY JAMES
THE DEATH OF IVAN ILYICH / LEO TOLSTOY
TALES OF BELKIN / ALEXANDER PUSHKIN
THE AWAKENING / KATE CHOPIN
ADOLPHE / BENJAMIN CONSTANT
THE COUNTRY OF THE POINTED FIRS / SARAH ORNE JEWETT
PARNASSUS ON WHEELS / CHRISTOPHER MORLEY
THE NICE OLD MAN AND THE PRETTY GIRL / ITALO SVEVO
LADY SUSAN / JANE AUSTEN
JACOB'S ROOM / VIRGINIA WOOLF
MRS. DALLOWAY / VIRGINIA WOOLF

THE ART OF THE NOVELLA

TITLES IN THE COMPANION SERIES
THE CONTEMPORARY ART OF THE NOVELLA

THE PATHSEEKER / IMRE KERTÉSZ
THE DEATH OF THE AUTHOR / GILBERT ADAIR
THE NORTH OF GOD / STEVE STERN
CUSTOMER SERVICE / BENOÎT DUTEURTRE
BONSAI / ALEJANDRO ZAMBRA
ILLUSION OF RETURN / SAMIR EL-YOUSSEF
CLOSE TO JEDENEW / KEVIN VENNEMAN
A HAPPY MAN / HANSJÖRG SCHERTENLEIB
SHOPLIFTING FROM AMERICAN APPAREL / TAO LIN
LUCINELLA / LORE SEGAL
SANDOKAN / NANNI BALESTRINI
THE UNION JACK / IMRE KERTÉSZ

THE CONTEMPORARY ART OF THE NOVELLA